Second printing edition
Paperback ISBN: 978-1-7781262-9-1

Other books by Christine can be found here:
https://www.cloganinsideinspiration.com

Contact: tinemusic3@hotmail.com

Why we need to protect owls

Saving owls will help save an entire ecosystem on which plant, other animals and humans depend. There won't be a proper balance in the food chain. If even one species of owl goes extinct, the rodent and prey population will grow at a fast rate. Over a single season, an owl will devour hundreds of rodents and other pests.

Burrowing owls, Blakiston's Fish owl and Barn owls are among the most endangered species. The Northern Spotted owl is the rarest.

The Nature Conservancy is working around the world to protect owls and owl habitat. In some places, they tag and track Snowy owls. In Washington, they protect the Spotted owl habitat by conserving old growth forests. They are finalizing a conservation strategy that reaches across more than 13 million acres of Thunder Basin and northward into Montana, which includes Burrowing owl habitat.

The Owl Research Institute is more than a conservation group. Besides climate issues, habitat loss and declining owl populations, they focus on understanding the causes behind the trends in the data. After 30 years of fieldwork and research, it's less about discovering owls and more about protecting their future.

(Quotes are from the Nature Conservancy Website and the Owl Research Institute Website)

Did you know?

- Owls have excellent vision and hearing

- They are more active at night (nocturnal)

- They help keep the rodent population down (this helps prevent disease and other problems)

- Owls are not afraid of much (maybe a flash of bright lighting or loud, sudden clapping from humans)

- Owls mate for life (very protective of their mate, babies and their hunting territory)

- Their eyes are tube-shaped

- Owls hide their food when hunting is good (it's called "cashing")

- An owl's home is called a "roost."

- There are 250 known species of owls in the world

HOOTIE
IS
AWESOME!

This is Hootie's human,

Landon.

Hootie has a few friends

he would like you to meet.

This is Blaire, and her human

is Lincoln.

This is Kitty.

Her human is Gabby.

Woo Hooo Hooo!

Hootie rides a bike
to move around.

Honestly, owls fly in the sky without a sound.

Human food can
be so much fun.

No, no Hootie,
this is how
it's done.
(Owls eat mice.)

Soccer with my friends;

Hootie wants to play.

No, no Hootie.

Owls play this way.

Is Hootie on the potty

where he should be?

No, no Hootie.

Like this, on a tree.

Owls regurgitate pellets with undigestible bones of small prey inside.

We wear glasses to
better see the screen.

Hootie, you don't
need glasses because your
eyesight is keen!

Easter egg hunting is so much fun.

Hootie looks dashing.

No, no Hootie.
Owls HIDE their
food when hunting
is good.
It's called "Cashing".

Drinking chocolate milk with my humans.

Wow! This is really neat.

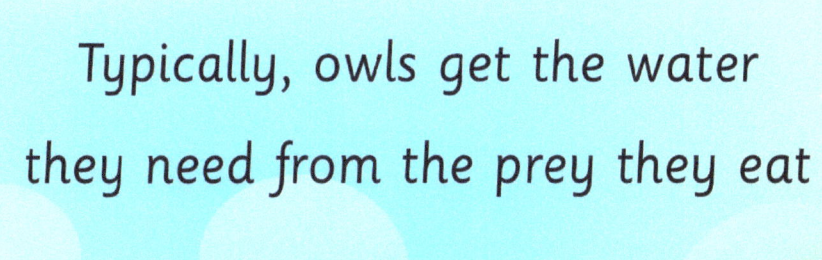

Typically, owls get the water they need from the prey they eat

or bathe.

Oh boy! This is not where
Hootie should be.

He should be in a barn
or here in a tree.

Open wide, if you please.

Christine J. Logan
Canadian Author

Gayatri Ray
Illustrator

Christine Logan is an experienced children's book author. She enjoys writing books that inspire a positive message. Everyone and everything around her, inspire her to write and share her books with us.

It's been amazing having input from my grandchildren about how they should look in the book and assist in the whole process of creating this book.

You can find Christine's books on Amazon as well as her author website: **www.cloganinsideinspiration.com**

Thank you, to everyone who inspires me and everyone who helps in the process of getting my books published.

Gayatri Ray, better known as **bigmonky** on Fiverr business platform.

Bigmonky Productions is a creative enterprise specializing in children's book illustration and animation. This is a husband and wife team with many years of experience creating illustrated children's books, storyboards, animation and educational videos for various companies and individuals.

Life is reflected in art, so let us bring your vision to life with our expertise and professionalism.

Quotes from my humans

"Hootie is the cutest, most cuddly owl. He sleeps beside me every night."

Landon

"Blaire is very, very, very cute. She loves to sleep."

Lincoln

"Kitty is white, brown and black. She is very cuddly and she likes to sleep with me."

Gabrielle

"I'm so proud of my grandchildren. It's wonderful to see the love and imagination they have and share with others."

Grandma

Lincoln, Landon and Gabby.

This book is blessed because you
helped create it. Thank you.

Love Grandma

www.ingramcontent.com/pod-product-compliance
Lightning Source LLC
Chambersburg PA
CBHW040901120626
46551CB00001B/114